AMAZING LAND ANIMALS

Thanks to the creative team:
Senior Editor: Alice Peebles
Fact checking: Kate Mitchell
Design: www.collaborate.agency

Original edition copyright 2016 by Hungry Tomato Ltd.

Hungry Tomato™
A division of Lerner Publishing Group, Inc.
241 First Avenue North
Minneapolis, MN 55401 USA

For reading levels and more information, look up this title at www.lernerbooks.com.

Main body text set in Mate Regular 10/12.

Library of Congress Cataloging-in-Publication Data

Names: Farndon, John, author. | Portolano, Cristina, illustrator.
Title: Amazing land animals / by John Farndon ; illustrated by Cristina Portolano.
Description: Minneapolis : Hungry Tomato, [2017] | Series: Animal bests | Audience: Ages 8-12. | Audience: Grades 4 to 6. | Includes index.
Identifiers: LCCN 2016003160 (print) | LCCN 2016009328 (ebook) | ISBN 9781512406276 (lb : alk. paper) | ISBN 9781512411690 (pb : alk. paper) | ISBN 9781512409215 (eb pdf)
Subjects: LCSH: Animal behavior—Juvenile literature. | Animal defenses—Juvenile literature. | Animal intelligence—Juvenile literature.
Classification: LCC QL751.5 .F37 2017 (print) | LCC QL751.5 (ebook) | DDC 591.5—dc23

LC record available at http://lccn.loc.gov/2016003160

Manufactured in the United States of America
1-39300-21137-3/29/2016

ANIMAL BESTS

AMAZING LAND ANIMALS

BY JOHN FARNDON
ILLUSTRATED BY CRISTINA PORTOLANO

HUNGRY TOMATO.

NO LARGE ANIMAL IS QUITE
AS GOOD AT LIVING IN THE
TREETOPS AS THE ORANGUTAN!

CONTENTS

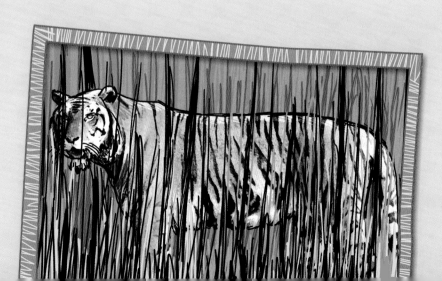

SMARTEST ANIMALS ON LAND

Some people think animals aren't very smart. They could not be more wrong. Nearly all animals are very good at what they were born to do—far better than humans. And they have special skills and characteristics that help them to survive. This book introduces you to some of the most amazing land animals.

Here's a taste of how amazing land animals are, before we even get on to the really clever stuff . . .

SPRINTERS

The fastest creature on land is the cheetah (above). It can run at speeds of up to 75 miles per hour (121 kilometers per hour) and accelerate to nearly 60 miles per hour (100 km/h) in three seconds.

HIGH JUMP

A little African antelope called the klipspringer (left) can jump nearly 25 feet (8 meters) in the air and land on a rock no bigger than a coin. This is because it stands on the tips of its hooves, making it a very agile rock climber.

LONG JUMP

Australia's red kangaroo (left) can cover 30 feet (9 m) in a single leap as it bounds along. It also jumps at speed, up to 35 miles per hour (56 km/h), and keeps this up for many miles without tiring. The tendons in its hind legs act like springs, pushing it into the next leap.

ALL—ROUNDER

The hare (right) is a super athlete of the animal world. It can run at speeds of up to 45 miles per hour (72 km/h) and leap nearly 13 feet (4 m) in a single bound.

HURDLING

In a steeplechase horse race, horses have to jump thirty or so fences well over 4.3 feet (1.3 m) tall, while running 3 miles (5 km). They are trained to save their energy as they race, so they will have a burst of speed when needed.

CLEVER!

Elephants have the biggest brains of any land animal. And the cortex, the part of the brain that does the clever thinking, is much bigger than ours. No other four-legged animal comes near elephants for doing clever things—using tools, learning, solving problems, remembering, playing, communicating, and feeling complex emotions.

THUMP CALL

When an elephant stamps its foot, the vibrations are felt far and wide. Other elephants can detect these vibrations more than 20 miles (32 km) away, through the soft soles of their feet or by touching their sensitive trunks to the ground. Scientists believe this is how elephants send messages and find each other. It is called seismic communication.

IT'S NOT A PROBLEM

Elephants are great problem solvers. Scientists found that when faced with food too high to reach, elephants worked out how to move a box and stand on it to get the food. In the 1970s, an elephant called Bandula even figured out how to undo a tricky Brummel lock holding the chains on her leg— and then showed other elephants how to do it, too!

Brummel Lock

SAYING GOODBYE

Elephants look after each other in a remarkable way. If one of them dies, the others give it a send-off that seems like a human funeral. They throw leaves over the body to cover it, and stand around it for days making sad noises as if to say goodbye.

ELEPHANT NURSERY

Elephants have a very strong social structure. Baby elephants need to be looked after for a long time, and all the herd help the mother do it. It's not because baby elephants are slow learners, but because they have so much to learn. They are entirely dependent on their mothers until the age of five, and may still need their mother's milk until they're ten.

JUMBO DA VINCI

Some elephants in Thailand paint pictures. They hold a brush in their trunk and paint on a canvas set up by their trainers. Critics say the elephants are being led by their trainers. Yet the elephants paint great pictures of trees, flowers, and other elephants, and some of their paintings now hang in art galleries.

GETTING THE MESSAGE

Like us, chimpanzees have big brains and hands that can grasp things and hold them up for a close look. Their eyes look to the front as ours do, and they have many similar facial expressions. They live in tightly knit social groups, and often greet each other by holding out hands, kissing, or hugging. They even smile and laugh. No wonder we think they're clever!

WASHOE

Washoe was an amazing chimp who was taught to use sign language developed for hearing impaired humans. She learned 350 words, including *shoe*, *clothes*, *me*, and *you*. She could have long conversations with her trainers in sign language. She didn't just use words she was taught. Faced with a thermos flask, Washoe signed, *metal cup drink*.

NOT FAIR!

Scientists tested capuchin monkeys by giving them a grape or a cucumber as a reward for handing the scientists a stone. When one monkey saw his mate getting a sweet grape while he only got a boring cucumber, he flung the cucumber back in protest.

HEY, GUYS!!!

Just like us, chimpanzees tell each other things using different sounds and facial expressions. They make a *pant-hoot* call to tell other chimps to join them for something exciting, such as finding a new fruit tree. They pant *oo-oo-oo* quicker and quicker, higher and higher, and louder and louder.

LAB CHIMPS

Because chimps are so like us, scientists often kept them in laboratories to experiment on. But because they are such social creatures, chimpanzees suffer when isolated from their friends and families. Fortunately, the worst of these experiments have been banned. But some chimps are still subjected to experiments.

NOW, LOOK HERE!

Chimpanzees can tell each other things by the way they move their hands and feet. We don't know what all these gestures mean. But recently, researchers at St. Andrews University in the United Kingdom worked out thirty-six of them. The researchers found the gestures for saying things like *Stop that!*, *Hug me*, and *Move away*.

"Climb on my back" (showing foot)

"Groom me here, please!" (touching body)

"Let's groom" (long scratching on body)

"Flirt with me" (stripping leaves)

"Move over" (little backhand nudge)

DETECTOR POWER

Bats may be small, but they're very clever. They are the only mammals that can really fly. And most bats also have a sound location system so precise they can use it to catch insects in mid-air—in pitch darkness! That's why most sleep safely in places like caves and trees in the day, and only hunt at night when there are fewer dangerous birds about.

I CAN HEAR YOU!

Most bats have very sharp hearing, which is how they find their way in the dark. They send out very high squeaks that bounce, or echo, off nearby objects. The echoes indicate where things are, what shape they are, and how they are moving. This echolocation system is so precise a bat can identify an insect in a split second.

)) = Emitted Sound Waves
(squeaks made by the bat)

)) = Returning Sound Waves

NURSERY FOR BATS

In some bat species, the mothers take their young with them when they go out hunting. In others, the babies are left huddled together in a vast nursery roost, looked after by a few nannies. Most of the mothers go out hunting. When they come back, they locate their young in the dark by their distinctive cries, and feed them.

HANGING OUT

Unlike birds, bats sleep hanging upside down. That's because their legs don't have the power for an upward take-off. By hanging upside down, they can just drop off and fly straight away. They can also sleep in places that are harder for predators to get at.

FINGER FLIGHT

Bats have hands with very long fingers. Their wings are sheets of very thin skin stretched between their fingers and attached to their legs. The skin is curved like an airplane's wing, so bats are even better fliers than most birds. To flap its wings and fly, a bat just waggles its fingers . . .

SUCKERS

The vampire bats of South and Central America feed on the blood of other animals. They have two very sharp fangs for puncturing skin. Typically, they pounce while the animal is asleep, making two little holes to release the blood. Then they lick the blood with their long tongue. Vampire bats are not the nasty creatures of horror movies. They are very caring animals who look after each other.

SUPER SENSES

Snakes have an amazing sense of smell. They can detect faint scents far away and pinpoint the direction of a scent—so they can sniff out prey while remaining hidden in dense undergrowth. And some snake species "see" with heat sensors.

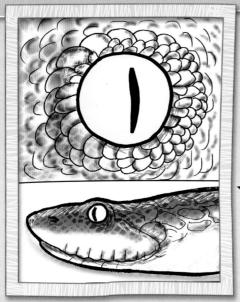

AMBUSH EYES

The dark center of an eye is called the *pupil*. In most animals, the pupil is round. But in a snake's eye it is a narrow slit. Scientists think the narrowing helps the snake to see better in the dark—like squinting. That way, a snake can keep its prey in focus without moving—perfect for an ambush!

LISTEN TO THE MUSIC

Snake charmers play a special kind of flute called a *pungi*. The music seems to hypnotize poisonous snakes, such as cobras, which sway with the pungi as it moves. In fact, it's all a trick. Snakes can't hear well enough to respond to music! They are just warily tracking the movements of what could be a predator.

HOTSPOT

If you thought thermal imaging was super-modern technology, think again. Some snakes have been using it for millions of years. Pythons, boas, and pit vipers have special pits in their snouts that can detect heat. With these pits, they can "see" heat and detect prey in complete darkness.

HOW DOES YOUR DOG SMELL?

It's no wonder that dogs go around sniffing. A huge percentage of their brain is devoted to smelling. And they have an area in their nose for scent detection that is seventeen times as big as ours. Bloodhounds can track the faint scent left by another animal up to ten days earlier. That's why police use dogs to help track down criminals or missing people.

HOW SNAKES SMELL WITH THEIR TONGUES

A snake's nostrils are only for breathing, not smelling. Snakes smell with their tongues. When a snake flicks out its forked tongue, it's actually smelling the air. The tongue collects scents and small organisms from the air, and takes them back into the snake's mouth. There the tongue's forks touch the snake's scent detector, which is called the Jacobson's organ.

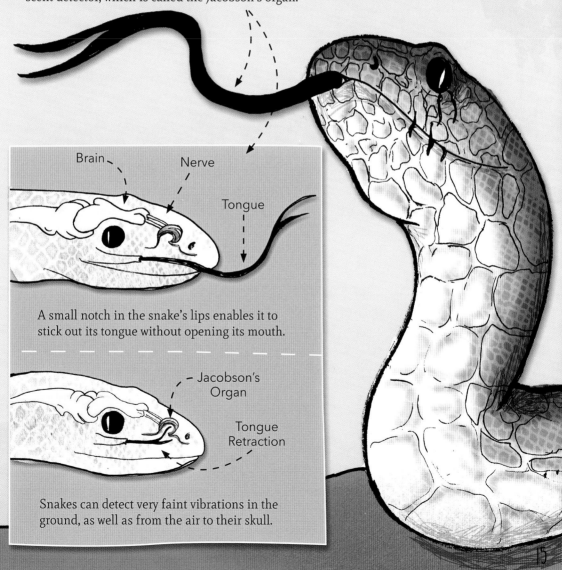

Brain

Nerve

Tongue

A small notch in the snake's lips enables it to stick out its tongue without opening its mouth.

Jacobson's Organ

Tongue Retraction

Snakes can detect very faint vibrations in the ground, as well as from the air to their skull.

VANISHING ACT

Some animals are very, very good at not being seen. They are colored and shaped so much like their surroundings that they seem to vanish. This is called camouflage. Tigers, giraffes, snakes, and chameleons use camouflage. But the master is the gecko: lizards that live in warm places. They are so good at hiding, some species may never have been seen!

TIGER, TIGER

Some animals are camouflaged to make them invisible when they're completely still. But a tiger's stripes make it hard to see when it's slinking through trees and long grass. All the unwary prey sees are flickering shadows . . . until it's too late. This kind of camouflage is called disruptive coloration. It breaks up the animal's outline, so only the stripes can be seen, not the telltale shape.

CAN'T SEE ME!

Geckos are the best vanishers of all. They take on the colors and patterns of their native forests to become almost invisible. The satanic leaf-tailed gecko can actually change color, from orange to green to brown to yellow, matching leaves and tree trunks. It's also shaped so much like a leaf that it's almost impossible to spot unless it moves!

TALL STORY

Giraffes have very bold checker-pattern markings but scientists are not sure why. Some say their disruptive coloration makes them less visible against the shifting shadows between trees. But an adult giraffe is so large it is hard to miss. It relies on size and strength to fend off hunting lions.

Eastern Coral Snake

Scarlet Kingsnake

WHO'S THE KILLER?

One way to avoid being attacked is to look like you're very dangerous. That's what the scarlet kingsnake (above) does. It's actually quite harmless. But its markings look very similar to the highly venomous eastern coral snake (top). So predators steer clear of the kingsnake, just in case!

COLOR COORDINATED

Chameleons are the best color changers of all. They change color to keep their bodies at the right temperature, to signal to other chameleons, and to hide. In a few minutes, a chameleon can turn from pink and purple to yellow and turquoise. To do this, they have two special layers of skin. Each contains crystals that absorb colors in sunlight in different ways.

17

BRILLIANT BUILDERS

Beavers are the animal world's most brilliant builders. To make a safe home, they build a dam of sticks and mud across a stream to create a pond. Then they build a little house, called a lodge, in the pond. The only ways in are through underwater tunnels, so predators can't get in. The lodge also keeps the beavers snug all winter.

TREE FELLERS

Beavers don't build dams just from loose sticks. They actually chop down large trees. They can gnaw through quite thick tree trunks with their strong teeth. After chopping down a tree, they strip off leaves and branches, before carrying the log away in their teeth. They may even build canals to float logs into place.

BUILDERS AT WORK

To create a dam, beavers work at night for safety. First they make a row of vertical sticks across the stream bed. Then they fill the gaps with horizontal sticks and mud. They carry sticks between their teeth, and mud and stones in their forepaws. Once the dam is complete (below, opposite page), they start work on the lodge (below), piling up logs, sticks, and mud into a cone around the underwater entrances.

BEAVER LODGE

Inside, the lodge stays quite warm, even in winter.

Two Underwater Entrances (one also opposite side)

Wall (about 3 feet (1 m) thick)

GORILLA NESTS

Only humans are better at building homes than beavers. But gorillas build large nests in the treetops to sleep safely in at night. The nests are up to 6.6 feet (2 m) across and made of sticks and grasses loosely knit together. These are short-term refuges, before the gorilla moves on to find food in another place.

BEAVER DIVERS

Beavers are rodents, like rats and mice. But they are adapted for living in water and for building. They have large, webbed hind feet and a huge flipperlike tail, perfect for swimming. Underwater, a transparent membrane protects their eyes, and flaps cover their nostrils and ears. Their front paws are like hands, so they can position sticks and mud with great skill. One other mammal has webbed feet and is equally equipped for living in rivers—the duck-billed platypus of Australia.

Duck-billed Platypus

Beaver

Pond is 6.6 feet (2 m) deep

 BEAVER DAM

PUZZLE MASTERS

People often think of rats as vicious, dirty pests. In fact, they are clever little creatures that care for each other in a remarkable way. They feed on all kinds of food, and their big brains help them figure out how to find it in all kinds of places. Because rats are so clever, they have learned to live in towns and cities in a way no other creature has.

RATS AND MAZES

Rats are super-clever at finding their way through mazes. This shows they can solve puzzles and have good memories. Scientists discovered their skill with mazes a century ago. Ever since, they have been testing rats with mazes to help find out how we humans learn things, and if our brains work in the same way.

DREAM ON

Rats can find their way through mazes in their sleep—literally. Scientists recently found that, when asleep, their brains fired in the same pattern as if they were going through a maze to find a treat. It seems that they dream about it!

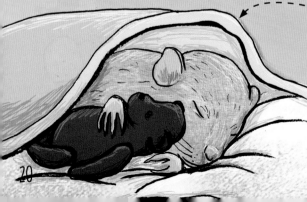

HERO RATS

In some areas in times of conflict, people hid dangerous land mines underground. African giant pouched rats, often nicknamed HeroRATS, can be trained to sniff out these mines so they can be safely destroyed. The rats are too light to set off the mines, but they can smell them and show their handlers where they are, in return for a food reward.

A RAT'S WHISKERS

A rat's whiskers are extraordinarily sensitive. When rats whisk their whiskers along surfaces, it gives them an incredibly detailed 3D picture of the surfaces. Whiskers can also detect faint air currents, and vibrations in the air. That's why rats can move around and find things in complete darkness.

CARING RATS

Far from being vicious, rats look after each other caringly. A few years ago, scientists conducted tests to show this. They put two rats inside a cage with a delicious chunk of chocolate. One of the rats was trapped inside a box. The other rat would not touch the chocolate until he had freed his friend from the box. Then the two ate the chocolate together.

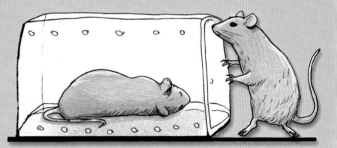

URBAN LEARNERS

Rats are not the only animals that have adapted to city life. Foxes have learned to find their way about the streets and find food there, too. So have raccoons. They are very clever at getting into places where food is locked away safely—or so people think. Raccoons have been seen opening jars, untying knots, picking locks, opening car latches, and even undoing special catches on garbage cans.

TOOL USERS

Orangutans are apes that live in the forests of Sumatra and Borneo in Southeast Asia. Like gorillas and chimpanzees, they are closely related to humans and very intelligent. They are among the few animals that can learn how to use new tools.

STAYING CLOSE TO MOM

Young orangutans stay close to their mothers for at least ten years after they are born—and even after that, often come home for a visit until they are sixteen years old. Only humans have such a long and close bond with their mothers. Orangutans need this because they have a lot to learn: where to find food, what to eat and how to use special tools to get food, and how to build a sleeping nest.

ORANGUTAN TOOLS

Like us, orangutans have hands, which makes it easy for them to use tools. But they don't just use tools— they learn to find new tools to use in new situations. For example, they use sticks to dig insects out of holes. But they don't always use the same kind of stick. They choose a different stick to suit the hole. Some orangutans even devise umbrellas when it rains!

MONKEY NUTCRACKERS

Capuchin monkeys live in South and Central America. They got their name from looking a little like Capuchin monks, who wear brown robes with large, light brown hoods. These clever animals also use tools. They crack open nuts, knocking them with rocks against a hard surface. But first they carefully position the nut so it is in the most stable position.

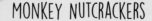

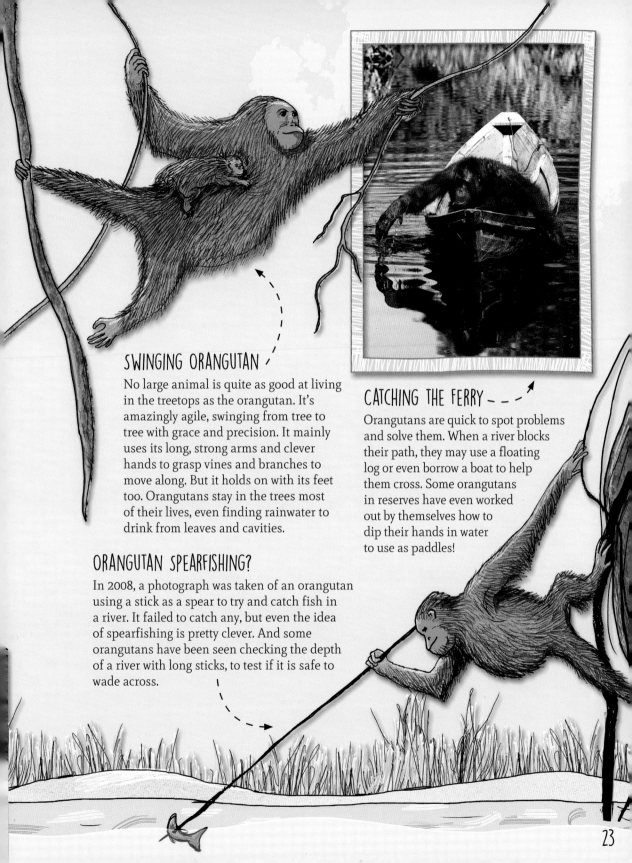

SWINGING ORANGUTAN

No large animal is quite as good at living in the treetops as the orangutan. It's amazingly agile, swinging from tree to tree with grace and precision. It mainly uses its long, strong arms and clever hands to grasp vines and branches to move along. But it holds on with its feet too. Orangutans stay in the trees most of their lives, even finding rainwater to drink from leaves and cavities.

ORANGUTAN SPEARFISHING?

In 2008, a photograph was taken of an orangutan using a stick as a spear to try and catch fish in a river. It failed to catch any, but even the idea of spearfishing is pretty clever. And some orangutans have been seen checking the depth of a river with long sticks, to test if it is safe to wade across.

CATCHING THE FERRY

Orangutans are quick to spot problems and solve them. When a river blocks their path, they may use a floating log or even borrow a boat to help them cross. Some orangutans in reserves have even worked out by themselves how to dip their hands in water to use as paddles!

23

STAYING ALIVE IN THE ARCTIC

Polar bears are uniquely suited to living in the cold of the Arctic, where the sea is frozen all year round, and temperatures are often -40°F (-40°C). Arctic foxes and caribou come to the Arctic too. But only the polar bear can live on the sea ice.

DINNER HOLE

Polar bears are the largest land predators, weighing up to 1,300 pounds (600 kilograms) and standing up to 10 feet (3 m) tall on their back legs. They feed mainly on ringed seals. They use their powerful sense of smell to find the breathing holes that seals cut in the ice. A bear then waits quietly and patiently for a seal to come up for air—and pounces.

LAYERS FOR WARMTH

A polar bear has two layers of fur. The top layer of long hairs keeps the bear warm and dry. This fur is covered in oil, so it's waterproof. The bottom layer of soft fur is like a woolly sweater trapping air to give insulation. Under the bear's skin is a thick layer of fat for extra warmth.

STRONG SWIMMERS

Polar bears move around on ice and land mostly by walking. But they often need to swim from one ice patch to another. They are very good swimmers, and the air trapped in their fur helps them keep afloat. Polar bears have been seen swimming more than 60 miles (100 km) from shore.

SNOW DEN

Unlike other bears, polar bears don't really hibernate in winter. But a pregnant female bear digs out a small den in the snow in the autumn. She crawls inside and waits for snow to bury the entrance. Then, snugly protected from the weather, she gives birth to her cubs. She emerges in spring when the cubs are strong enough to make the journey to the sea ice.

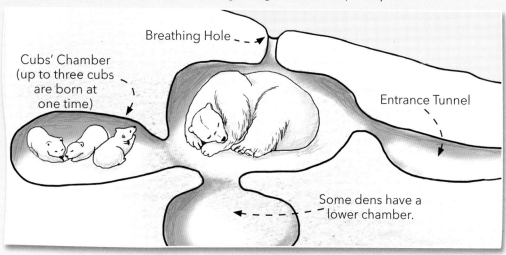

Breathing Hole

Cubs' Chamber (up to three cubs are born at one time)

Entrance Tunnel

Some dens have a lower chamber.

WHITE FOR WINTER

Arctic foxes have shorter ears and noses than other foxes so they lose less heat from them. In winter, their beautiful white fur makes them almost invisible against the snow and helps keep them safe from polar bears. When the snow melts in spring, their fur turns brown, so they are just as hard to see.

THE LONG TREK

One way to live in the Arctic is to get away from it in winter. Each autumn, vast herds of caribou make the long trek south, up to 930 miles (1,500 km) one-way. The next spring, as the weather eases, they will head back north where they can safely give birth to their young.

DESERT SURVIVORS

Often scorching hot, and with little food and water, deserts are tough! Some foxes, rodents, tortoises, and lizards can live here. But the master survivor is the camel, which can get by for a long time without any food and water at all, by storing fat in its hump and water in its stomach lining.

EXTRAORDINARY CAMEL

A camel can last a week or more without water, then drink as much as 32 gallons (46 liters) at one time to top up. They can also survive for several months without food, gradually using the fat stored in their hump for energy.

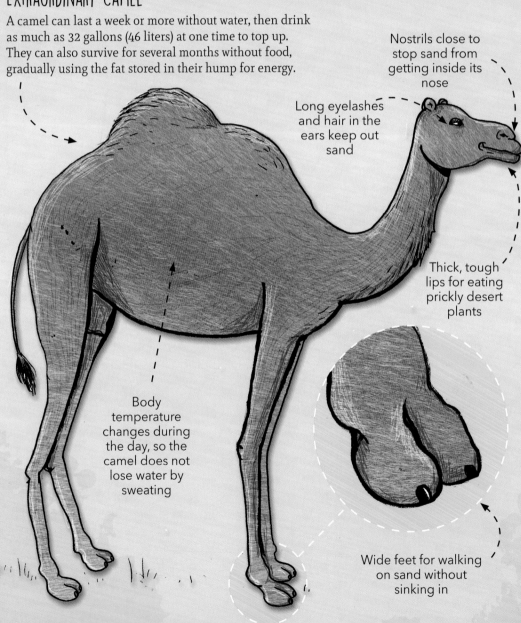

Nostrils close to stop sand from getting inside its nose

Long eyelashes and hair in the ears keep out sand

Thick, tough lips for eating prickly desert plants

Body temperature changes during the day, so the camel does not lose water by sweating

Wide feet for walking on sand without sinking in

BACTRIAN CAMEL

There are two kinds of camel: the one-humped Dromedary of the Middle East and northwest Africa; and the two-humped Bactrian of Central Asia. The Bactrian has had to survive the freezing winters of the Gobi Desert—its original home—so it has a thick, shaggy coat.

COOL STRATEGIES

Every desert creature has its own clever technique for surviving in the desert by keeping cool and collecting water.

TRAPPING MOISTURE

The fierce spikes of Australia's thorny devil lizard don't just save it from predators. They catch the dew that settles in the night and provide it with a source of water.

LOSING HEAT

The tiny fennec fox of the Sahara has giant ears that radiate heat away very quickly and keep it cool. It also has big paws for scooping out shady burrows in the sand.

KEEPING WATERED

The kangaroo rat lives in the deserts of the southwestern United States. It never has to drink water—it gets all the water it needs from eating seeds.

DIGGING DOWN

To survive the heat, the desert tortoise spends most of the time in burrows underground. It digs pools to catch any rain.

27

THE BEST OF THE BEST

ELEPHANTS
SPECIES: Two (African and Asian)
LIVE IN: Mainly grassland (African); mainly forest (Asian)
EAT: Grasses, small plants, bushes, fruit, twigs, tree bark, and roots

The African elephant is the largest land animal, at about 6.6 tons (6 tonnes). It eats up to 660 pounds (300 kg) of food every day!

CHIMPANZEES
SPECIES: One
LIVE IN: Central African forests and woods
EAT: Plants, fruit, insects, and even lizards and frogs

Chimps have much stronger arms and legs than humans, continually developed by climbing and swinging through the trees. They run on all fours.

BATS
SPECIES: More than 1,300
LIVE IN: Everywhere on land but very cold places
EAT: 70 percent of bats eat fruit, most of the rest eat insects

More than 1,000 bat species are nocturnal, sleeping during the day and hunting at night.

SNAKES
SPECIES: Close to 3,000
LIVE IN: Everywhere on land but Antarctica
EAT: Small animals

Many snakes, such as cobras and vipers, have venomous fangs for stunning or killing their prey. Others, such as pythons and boas, are constrictors that wrap around their prey and crush them.

GECKOS
SPECIES: 1,500
LIVE IN: Warm places
EAT: Insects

A gecko can lose its tail to escape an attack, and then grow it back. The eyes of nocturnal geckos are 350 times more sensitive to colors than ours.

BEAVERS
SPECIES: Two (North American and Eurasian)
LIVE IN: Streams in cool woods
EAT: Water plants in summer, woody plants in winter

Beavers are the second largest rodents in the world, after capybaras. The beaver was hunted almost to extinction in Europe but is now being reintroduced.

RATS
SPECIES: 66
LIVE IN: Everywhere on land but Antarctica
EAT: Anything, including fruit, nuts, grain, and food waste

Rats are rodents, usually bigger than mice, with long tails. Those that live in cities are black rats and brown rats, which originally came from Asia.

ORANGUTANS
SPECIES: Two
LIVE IN: Borneo and Sumatra
EAT: Mostly fruit but also young leaves, shoots, bark, insects, honey, and birds' eggs

There are only about 60,600 in the world, mainly because humans have destroyed their forest homes to make farms and plantations.

POLAR BEARS
SPECIES: One
LIVE IN: Arctic coasts and ice floes
EAT: Mainly seals, also fish, seabirds, berries, and leaves

Because polar bears live much of their lives on sea ice, they are very vulnerable to global warming. There are only 26,000 left in the wild.

CAMELS
SPECIES: Two (the Dromedary (Africa and Middle East) and Bactrian (Central Asia))
LIVE IN: Deserts
EAT: Thorny plants, bushes, seeds, fish, and dried grass

Camels are born without humps, but grow them as they get older. They can live for forty-five years.

SPECIAL SKILLS

As with the animals featured in this book, there are many that have a skill that's so special and so much more amazing than anything humans could do. With many animals on land, that skill is hunting, and it's something that dogs and cats are especially good at.

LAUGHING HYENAS

In some movies, hyenas are shown as silly animals, because of the laughing sound they make. But they are really very clever hunters that pursue and kill much bigger animals, such as wildebeest. They do this by working together to isolate their prey and tire them out. When scientists conducted tests for learning skills that involved cooperation, hyenas were much quicker than chimpanzees. Who's laughing now!

WOLF FAMILIES

No animals look after each other as wolves do. They live in packs of up to ten, and each member makes sure the whole pack is all right. Sometimes a wolf will put itself in great danger to save the others. They all look after the pups, bringing them food and watching them while the others hunt. These close bonds really pay off when they go hunting big animals, such as moose. And a wolf howls to send messages, not to moan about the cold.

TIGER STRIPES

Tigers are the most formidable hunters of all. They have been known to hunt crocodiles, leopards, and pythons—all scary animals themselves. They can run up to 40 miles per hour (64 km/h), despite their immense size. They are very, very strong—a swipe from a tiger's paw can smash a cow's skull. Tigers can jump 16 feet (5 m) in the air. And they can swim.

DOG SENSE

Dogs have been our closest animal companions for tens of thousands of years, and it is easy to take them for granted. But they are also very clever. Some scientists think they are as clever as a two-year-old human. This means that dogs can understand as many words and signs as a two-year-old. But maybe that's not a good measure of how clever they are, since a dog isn't that interested in learning words. What dogs are very, very clever at is reading human body language. That's why they make such good friends.

KING OF THE HUNTERS

Lions aren't very fast. In fact, they're quite lazy. Yet they catch some of the world's fastest animals, such as the wildebeest, which can run at 50 miles per hour (80 km/h) for long periods. So how do lions do it? The answer is by stealth. Lions sneak from bush to bush, then suddenly spring. They're even better at lying in wait hiding—then they also have time for a snooze.

FAST FOOD

Cheetahs have the advantage of being the fastest runners on Earth, but they can only keep up the pace over short distances. So they have to get very close to their prey before making a move. That's why they're also amazingly good at creeping through grass unseen, using the layout of the land to stay low and out of sight, until the right moment for the final sprint.

INDEX

THE AUTHOR

John Farndon is Royal Literary Fellow at Anglia Ruskin University in Cambridge, United Kingdom, and the author of a huge number of books for adults and children on science, technology, and nature, including international best-sellers. He has been shortlisted four times for the Royal Society's Young People's Book Prize.

THE ILLUSTRATOR

Cristina Portolano was born in Naples, Italy, and studied in Bologna and Paris, graduating in Comics and Illustration. Her artwork has appeared in Italian magazines and comic books such as *Delebile* and *Teiera*. She lives and works in Bologna, and her first book has recently been published by Topipittori.

Picture Credits (abbreviations: t = top; b = bottom; c = center; l = left; r = right)
© www.shutterstock.com:

2 cl, 6 cl, 6 bl, 7 tl, 7 cr, 7 bl, 9 tl, 11 tl, 12 br, 13 tl, 15 tr, 17 tr, 17 cr, 19 tr, 21 br, 23 tr, 25 cl, 25 bl, 27 tl, 30 tl, 30 cr, 30 bl, 31 tl, 31 cr, 31 bl, 32 cr.